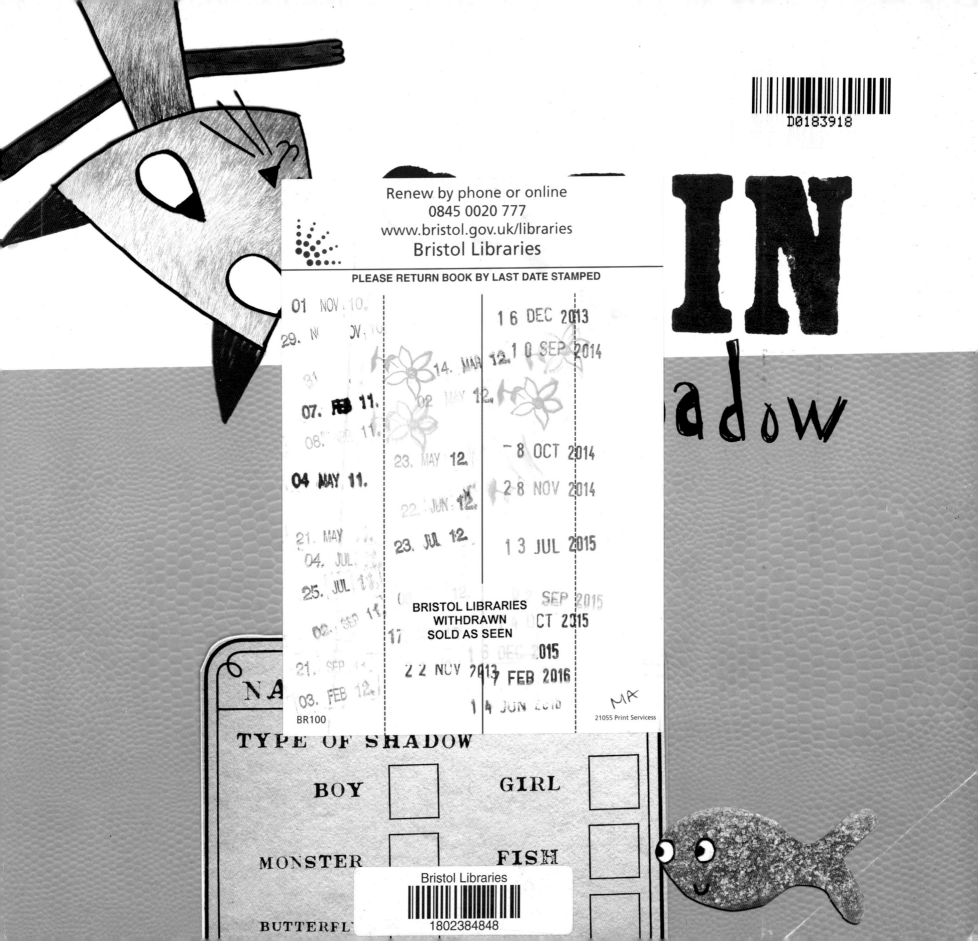

IN

adow

NAME

TYPE OF SHADOW

BOY

GIRL

MONSTER

FISH

BUTTERFLY

D0183918

FOR the TWO Hodgkinsons

WHo are

(without a SHADOW of a doubt)

SHINY & BRIGHT.
(FACT.)

To find out more about Leigh go to:
www.wonkybutton.com

ORCHARD BOOKS
338 Euston Road, London NW1 3BH
Orchard Books Australia
Level 17/207 Kent Street, Sydney, NSW 2000

First published in 2008 by Orchard Books
First published in paperback in 2009
ISBN 978 1 84616 629 7

Text and illustrations © Leigh Hodgkinson 2008
The right of Leigh Hodgkinson to be identified as the author and
illustrator of this work has been asserted by her in accordance
with the Copyrights, Designs and Patents Act, 1988.

A CIP catalogue record for this book is available
from the British Library.

2 4 6 8 10 9 7 5 3 1
Printed in China
Orchard Books is a division of Hachette Children's Books,
an Hachette UK company.
www.hachette.co.uk

COLIN

and the
Wrong shadow

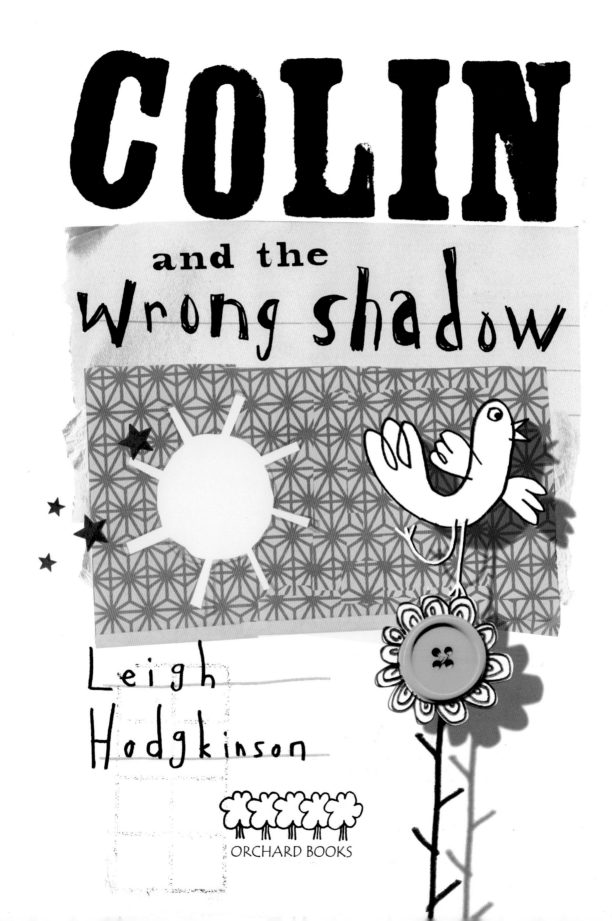

Leigh
Hodgkinson

ORCHARD BOOKS

Colin

has just woken up from his catnap. He smiles as he remembers his dream . . .

swimming

in a **gigantic** bowl of creamy milk.

Now that he is wide awake, Colin is feeling funny. Not funny ha ha but funny PECULIAR.

Colin has a feeling that things aren't quite as they should be...

For some reason, he appears to have the

Wrong shadow!

Colin has no idea why, but decides not to let a silly thing like this . . .

spoil an otherwise pleasant afternoon.

As it turns out, Colin's afternoon is NOT at all pleasant. The other cats

snigger.

Little Flossy Fluffball SQUEAKS at him.

The beaky birds don't **bother** to look up from their

SPLASHY bath.

Colin is starting to wonder if he **actually** is a **mouse** after all?

He does like the **odd** nibble of cheese, if that means anything?

Colin thinks that if he had any other shadow –

PERHAPS something

with a little more

WOW!

BUT it isn't in the least bit

hunky-dory.

Not in the slightest.

HOWEVER,

even GLOOMY cats need to stretch their legs occasionally. A good job too, as this is when Colin spies something VERY interesting indeed . . .

HIS OWN
SHADOW!

Look at it

skipping past

without a care in the WORLD.

WHAT
A CHEEK!

Colin decides to follow it.

He slinks snoopily under there . . .

He tippy-tappy toes over here . . .

Being ever so shushy and quiet as a . . .

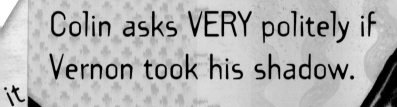

Colin asks VERY politely if Vernon took his shadow.

Vernon says,

"NO. Not exactly."

Colin thinks that SOMEONE is telling a tiny lie.

Hmmm...

Colin would rather like the
switch-SWAP switched BACK!

Colin asks VERY politely if Vernon took his shadow.

Vernon says,

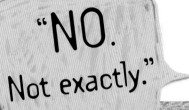 "NO. Not exactly."

Colin thinks that SOMEONE is telling a tiny lie.

Vernon gulps and says, "While you were snoozing your shadow got BORED and FIDGETY and wandered off."

VERNON thinks that **RIGHT NOW** would probably be a good time to scurry home.

UH-OH!

Colin's shadow is far too **BIG** to fit through the door.

Vernon squishes, **SQUEEZES** and <u>SQUASHES</u> it→

but it JUST WON'T BUDGE!

...then WHAT IS THE POINT?

You see it's JUST not EASY being a tiny pink mouse all of the time.

And having Colin's MARVELLOUS shadow meant that **EVERYBODY** took Vernon seriously for a change.

"You couldn't POSSIBLY ever understand, Colin,"

Vernon squeaks oh-so-quietly.

Colin knows **EXACTLY** how it feels, as it happens.

It's not nice to be sniggered at, SQUEAKED at and IGNORED, you know.

It made Colin feel TERRIBLY small and all alone.

Perhaps if they BOTH stopped worrying about silly shadows they could concentrate on more important things – like

having fun together!

First things first, to get Vernon out of this pickle!

Vernon PUSHES

and the shadow

until suddenly . . .

PING

toppily

... and Colin **PULLS**

STRETCHES...

tumble
bump.

PHEW-EE! Not exactly easy-peasy

but the result is SPOT-ON!

Vernon loves being footloose and fancy-free again

and has a new SPRING in his step.

This is because being with

BOTH

his own

shadow

AND

Colin

means

DOUBLE the fun!

In fact, Vernon
feels even

BETTER

than a SUPERSTAR.

More like a

SUPER-DOOPER-
STAR!

And to be honest,
lugging that big bulky
shadow about was a touch tiring.

"Perhaps a refreshing cuppa followed by a little snooooze will do the trick?"

Now, that is what Colin calls a pretty perfect plan!
One slurpy sip later, Colin clambers up onto his favourite cushion.

This time, his shadow is sleepy **too** and sticking like glue, so there will be

NO

prowling about

and getting into trouble with a certain

cheeky

little

mouse.